Fergus
221B Baker Street

and

The Case of Hickory, Dickory, Dock

written by

Gene G. Bradbury

illustrated by

Victoria Wickell-Stewart

BookWilde
Children's Books

MW00615657

Fergus of 221B Baker Street

The Case of Hickory, Dickory, Dock

Copyright: 2016 by Gene G. Bradbury

ISBN: 978-0-9971764-1-4

Printed in the USA by Createspace Independent Publishing Platform

Book prepress: Kate Weisel, weiselcreative.com

All inquiries should be addressed to

BookWilde Children's Books
422 Williamson Rd.
Sequim, WA 98382

BookWilde
Children's Books

Author's Dedication

For mystery readers of all ages,
but especially for those children
who wonder and ask, why?

~ Gene G. Bradbury

Illustrator's Dedication

To Pat Doran, my dearest friend.
Always with me in spirit as in presence.
And for Chloe for having such a loving Gramma.
Hugs to you.

~ Victoria Wickell-Stewart

Hickory, dickory, dock.

The mouse ran up the clock.

The clock struck one,

The mouse ran down,

Hickory, dickory, dock.

Everyone knows that 221B Baker Street is the home of the famous detective, Sherlock Holmes.

But did you know that it is also the home of Fergus's uncle, Delbert Mouse?

On a visit to England, Fergus crawled through a hole in the wall and found himself in the study of Mr. Holmes.

Over Mr. Holmes' desk was a lovely old clock. Near the clock stood a coat rack with the detective's famous deerstalker hat.

Fergus scurried back to Uncle Delbert's apartment.

In a hole in the wall of the apartment Fergus found a scribbled page. So began the mystery called, "The Case of Hickory, Dickory, Dock."

Fergus carried
the page
to Mr. Holmes'
study.

**At the top of the page was the poem,
"Hickory, Dickory, Dock."**

∽ Hickory Dickory Dock ∽

Why did the mouse run up the clock
and down again? Sherlock Holmes

**At the bottom of the page was a question
in Mr. Holmes' handwriting: "Why did the mouse
run up the clock and down again?"**

Fergus scratched
his head.
He pushed back
his deerstalker cap
and stared at
the clock.
"Why was
the mouse
in the clock?"
he squeaked.

Fergus's whiskers began to twitch. Someone was watching him!

On a nearby chair slept a yellow-eyed cat with sharp claws. It was Baskerville, the cat named after Sherlock Holmes' most famous case.

Fergus ducked behind the
pipe stand on
Mr. Holmes' desk.

Fergus held
his breath as
Baskerville
slipped from
the chair.

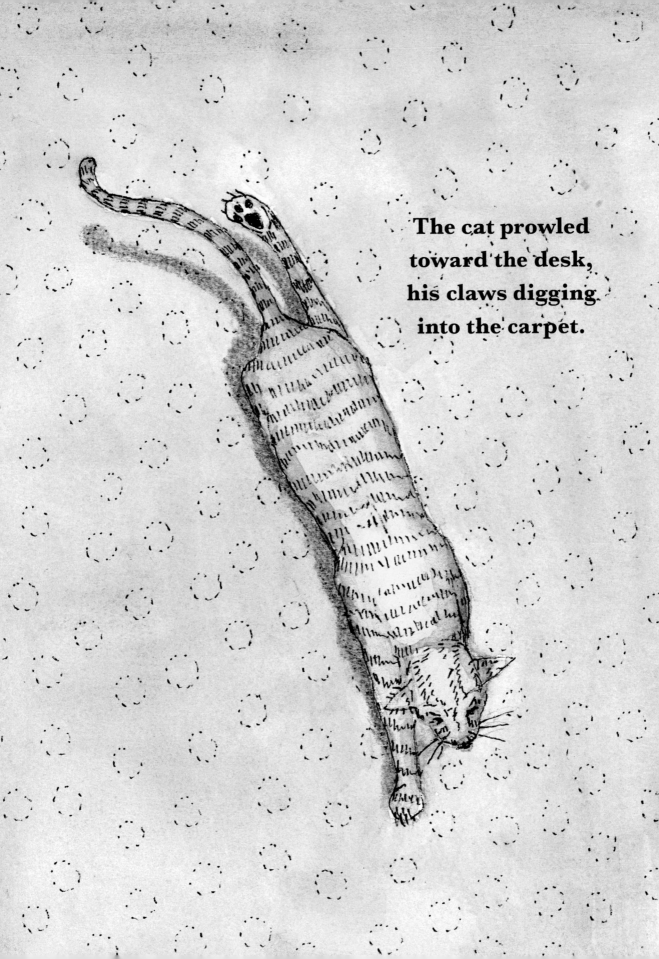

The cat prowled
toward the desk,
his claws digging
into the carpet.

**At that moment Uncle Delbert
appeared in the room.**

Baskerville sprang toward Uncle Delbert.

Uncle Delbert escaped through a hole in the wall.

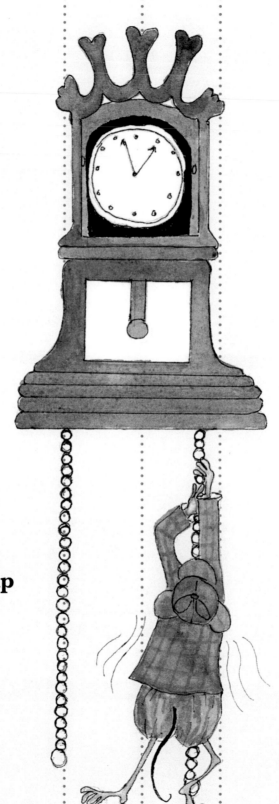

**Fergus ran up
the clock.**

Inside the clock,
Fergus saw
Baskerville's
yellow eyes
staring up at him.

Tick tock, tick tock,
tick tock.

The hands of the clock
moved toward one.

Baskerville waited
below, licking his lips.

The clock's gears
began to grind,
ready to
strike the hour.

Baskerville
moved toward
the clock's chains.

**The cat's teeth gleamed white
and his fur stood on end.**

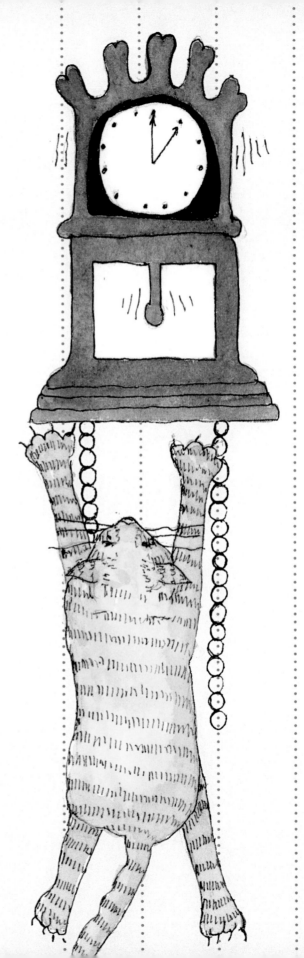

**BONG! The clock
chimed and Baskerville
sprang forward.**

**Fergus ran down
the clock, jumped to
the floor, and scurried
through the hole
in the wall.**

In his room Fergus lay on his bed
to catch his breath.
He had found the answer to Mr. Holmes' question.

The case of Hickory, Dickory, Dock
proved to be no mystery at all!
Fergus **knew** why the mouse ran up the clock
and down again.

All About Sherlock Holmes

1. Sherlock Holmes was a fictional detective created by the author Arthur Conan Doyle.

2. There is a Sherlock Holmes museum in London, England.

3. Sherlock Holmes' friend in solving mysteries was Dr. Watson.

4. Arthur Conan Doyle published his first story about Sherlock Holmes in 1887.

5. The most famous case of Sherlock Holmes is "The Hound of Baskervilles."

6. The stories of Sherlock Holmes have been translated into hundreds of languages.

7. Sherlock Homes is often recognized by his pipe and deerstalker hat.

8. Mr. Holmes is often seen at his window playing the violin.

9. Arthur Conan Doyle based much of the character of Holmes on professor Dr. Joseph Bell.

10. Sherlock Holmes' nemesis, or enemy, was Professor James Moriarty.

11. The four novels and 56 stories about Holmes are told by Mr. Holmes' friend, Dr. Watson.

12. Arthur Conan Doyle also wrote a book called **The Lost World** about dinosaurs still alive on an island, which inspired the movies *Jurassic Park* and *The Lost World*.

13. There are many Sherlock Holmes stories written just for kids. Check with your local library.

Fergus has had many
adventures.

BookWilde Children's Books

Children's Books by the Author

These books are illustrated by watercolorist Victoria Wickell-Stewart.

THE MOUSE WITH WHEELS IN HIS HEAD: Meet Fergus who wants to be the first mouse to ride the new Ferris Wheel at the World's Fair. Can a tiny mouse find a way to hitch a ride without being discovered? Follow Fergus's adventure at the 1893 Chicago Exhibition.

THE MOUSE WHO WANTED TO FLY: Adventure is in Fergus's blood. His success in riding the Ferris Wheel is in the past. When Fergus learns that two brothers, Orville and Wilbur, are going to fly the first powered airplane, Fergus is eager for a new adventure. Is it possible that a mouse can be on the first flight at Kitty Hawk?

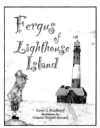

FERGUS OF LIGHTHOUSE ISLAND: Fergus, unlike his great uncle, isn't brave at all. He isn't looking for adventure. But when a hurricane threatens Lighthouse Island, adventure finds him. What will Fergus decide when the hurricane threatens the residents of Mouse Village? It's no place for a mouse who is afraid.

MISCHIEVOUS MAX, A TEDDY BEAR STORY: In Leon's room you will find many teddy bears. Most of them are soft and wonderful to take to bed. But there is one bear who Leon never takes to bed. His name is Max Bear and his fur tickles and his eyes are beastly. Leon knows something else about Max Bear. What if Leon tries sleeping with Max Bear for just one night? Would that be so bad? Leon is about to find out.

THE STAR TREE: "Do the forest animals know about Christmas?" asks Jody. With her grandfather, Jody goes into the forest to the place where the animals gather on Christmas Eve. Jody discovers that the world is a beautiful place to live. The Star Tree invites children to look for Christmas in the natural world.

THE KING'S BUTTERFLY invites children to enjoy and respect the beautiful Monarch Butterfly. When the King and Queen capture the butterfly to keep it for a royal pet, they soon find out that a butterfly is meant to fly free. Will they set the butterfly free that it might return again the next year? Perhaps Wizdrop the Wizard has the answer.

FERGUS OF 221B BAKER STREET *and The Case of Hickory, Dickory, Dock:*
Haven't you always wanted to know why the mouse ran up the clock? Of course, it's a mystery.
When Fergus, the adventuresome mouse, visits his uncle in England he comes to the right
place. Uncle Delbert lives behind the walls of the very house where Sherlock Holmes, the
famous detective, lives. With his deerstalker hat and Mr. Homes' magnifying glass, Fergus
sets out to solve the mystery. But there is one thing Fergus does not count on.

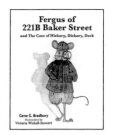

⋙━◆━⋘

WHEN CRICKETS SNORE is a delightful look at the private life of those singing
crickets. It's based on what Henry David Thoreau tells us . . .
   In the morning the crickets snore, in the afternoon they chirp, at midnight they dream.
Do they really snore? Page through the lovely illustrations by Jean Wyatt and see for yourself.
But read quietly, as the crickets may be in their pajamas.

⋙━◆━⋘

These books are illustrated by Hannah Bradbury.

CLOUD CLIMBER: What were his parents thinking, leaving him for three boring
weeks at his grandparent's farm? There would be no internet or cable television and what was
worse, only Cousin Emily for company. But on a trip to town with his grandfather, Seth learns
of Three Friends Hill and the Banshee's Cave. Are these linked to the discovery of a giant kite
Seth and Emily find in the old barn? The three weeks literally fly past and the cousins find that
Boring Farm is not so boring after all.

BEDTIME STORIES TO MAKE YOU SMILE: Bedtime Stories To Make
You Smile is the first in a series of bedtime books for young children. In this collection of
seven stories the intent is to bring a smile to the reader and send them to sleep with happy
dreams. Meet William, a bee who doesn't want to be a bee, and Mr. Mouse who loves to
read. You will puzzle over what Leonard has in his box, and delight when you hear of Willie
Snooze's special pillows. Aunt Bessie's Elephants may scare you, but just a little. You'll find
Boxcar Basset hurtling down the tracks, but not alone. A goldfish tale illustrates that safe
driving has benefits for everyone.

All Gene G. Bradbury books are available
through amazon.com, barnesandnoble.com and other retail outlets.

FACES FROM A BROKEN STAR, Short Stories

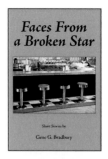

There was a time when traveling across country one might pull into any small town in America and find a mom and pop cafe. It was a good place to order a fried chicken dinner. Farmers gathered there to compare crop prices and check the weather before working in the field. The local café has disappeared. In these stories you're invited to meet the regulars at the Broken Star Cafe. Some of the characters may sound familiar. Others who will make you laugh and cry.

Poetry Books by Gene G. Bradbury

TRAVELING IN COMPANY

We never travel on our journey alone, but are linked by birth to others. They have walked before us and we follow in their footsteps. Those we come to know best on our travels we call family. From them we learn how to live. Others we meet along the way may lead us to quiet paths of reflection and spiritual practice. In this book of poems the author invites us to look at the many ways we are influenced by others as we travel together.

QUIET PLACES, MORNING WALKS:

Notes Between Secular and Sacred

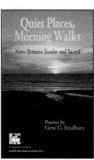

In this book of poetry the author invites the reader to find time each day for quiet and reflection. Each poem is a poetic response to a Psalm verse. The Psalm itself is rewritten in haiku. The book of poetry is prefaced with *morning litanies* to begin the day. The book ends with *evening songs* to end the day. The collection of verse can be used in the morning or evening as a time of quiet and devotion.

SAUNTERING WITH THOREAU

These poems begin with the author's love of Henry David Thoreau's Journals. Each poem is a reflection on a single quote by Thoreau. The poetry is a brief walk with the nineteenth century naturalist through the woods and along the rivers of Concord. Each poem invites the reader to look intently at the things around them and appreciate the place where they live. In Thoreau's words we are invited to find the kernel of life and not just the husk.

LET ME BE YOUR SERVANT, 100 REFLECTIVE MOMENTS

is both memoir and devotional reading. The book contains 100 short readings from long years of service in parish ministry, hospital chaplaincy, police chaplaincy, prison chaplaincy, and college chaplaincy. Each page reveals the author's choice of reading and thoughts about what it means to live in family and community.

BookWilde Children's Books

**All books available at Amazon.com
or barnesandnoble.com**

Made in the USA
San Bernardino, CA
22 June 2016